CONTENTS

JASPER
SPACE DOG!

Hilary Robinson

Illustrated by Lewis James

STRAUSS HOUSE PRODUCTIONS

3 8002 02419 655 4

For Benjamin & Isabella — HR

For Chris Mason – LJ

STRAUSS HOUSE PRODUCTIONS

www.strausshouseproductions.com

Editor: Jackie Walter
Publishing Assistant: Megan Brownrigg

Consultants
Janet Gough, Teaching and Learning Consultant - English and Literacy
Dr Suzie Imber, Associate Professor of Planetary Science, University of Leicester

With thanks to Kirsty Fenn, Michelle Ackroyd, Leeds SLS
Pauline McMahon, Claudia Cotton, Whitefield Primary School, Liverpool
Julie Allen, Birkwood Primary School, Cudworth, S Yorkshire
Sophie Robinson, Hugh Myddelton Primary School, Islington
Paul Watson, North Ormesby Primary Academy, Middlesbrough
Emma Wilkie, Broadfield Primary Academy, Crawley, Sussex
Wendy Mitchell, Wakefield SLS

Paperback: **ISBN-13: 978-1999338909**

A CIP catalogue record for this title is available from the British Library

Printed and bound in the UK.

CHAPTER 1
Cheesy Moon

The following pages are

TOP SECRET!

They are private letters between Charlie Tanner, Jasper and a rocket scientist.

Please do not share with anyone except your dog, cat, rabbit, hamster or ostrich.
Signed: Charlie Tanner and Jasper

Parrot

Jasper

Charlie

Secret letters!

Dr Isabella Starr
Rocket Scientist
Explore Space, UK

Dear Dr Starr,

My name is Charlie Tanner.
My dog, Jasper, and I would
like to ask you a few things
about the space mission,
Apollo 11, and the first moon
landing in July 1969.

We have a few questions
about the three astronauts
who made history too.

Jasper is thinking about the idea of becoming a space dog.

Our parrot, who is called Parrot, thinks it's all a big joke. Jasper is not put off by what Parrot thinks. Jasper has got some space boots which he wears in Bogna Park.

Lots of people have said – and Jasper says he has heard this too from other dogs in Bogna Park – that

the moon is made of cheese.

If the moon is made of cheese, do you know if the first astronauts to walk on the moon brought any moon cheese back with them? Jasper says there might be moon-cows on it because cheese is made from milk.

We would like to know this because I'd like to grate moon cheese on my pasta. Jasper would like to try a bit too (even though he's not a cheese fan). If they found the moon was made of cheese, then what type of cheese was it?

Did the astronauts give it a name such as Cheddar Moon and was it blue?

Jasper thinks a good name for moon cheese would be Lunar Blue.

We think that if the moon
is made of blue cheese then
it must be a type of cheese
which doesn't go mouldy. No
one has ever seen a mouldy
moon.

We would know this because mouldy bits of blue cheese would be pouring down on Earth like rain. Mouldy blue rain!

Jasper thought the rain
might smell like old socks too.

From Charlie Tanner, age 8
and a half, and Jasper, age 2
and a bit, but we're not sure
because he came from a rescue
centre and they didn't know.

Dear Charlie Tanner,

Thank you for asking whether the astronauts on the Apollo 11 mission found the moon was made of cheese.

They found, in fact, that the moon is made of rock. Much work was done before they left Earth so that they could be certain of a safe moon landing.

It would not have been advisable to land on cheese, especially if the moon was made of soft cheese!

Pieces of 'goodwill moon rock' were given to the nations of the world by the President of America.

Best wishes,
Dr Isabella Starr
Rocket Scientist

CHAPTER 2
Flying Hotdogs

Dr Isabella Starr
Rocket Scientist
Explore Space, UK

Dear Isabella,

(I hope you don't mind us calling you Isabella.) **WOW!** We would love to have received a piece of 'goodwill moon rock' in the post! We have another question, well, Jasper does ...

did the astronauts
eat hotdogs?

Hotdogs are Jasper's
favourite food, only he doesn't
like tomato sauce, but I do.
He doesn't like onions either
because he says they make
his breath smell! He has read
somewhere that the astronauts
ate hotdogs.

Jasper wants to know if sausages cooked in space fly about the rocket and if they are difficult to catch?

He seems to find the thought of a flying sausage funny. (I think he has been spending too much time with other dogs with daft ideas and I'm sure that Parrot thinks that too.)

Jasper also wants to know if the astronauts saw any dinosaurs on the moon or flying saucers? He really means UFOs – Unidentified Flying Objects. He is wondering if they saw any UFBs – Unidentified Flying Dog Bowls – out there as well?

From Charlie Tanner, age 8
and a half, and Jasper, age
2 and a bit, but he acts a
lot older usually, unless he's
mixing with other dogs in
Bogna Park and then he gets
really silly.

Dear Charlie Tanner,

First, the astronauts definitely didn't see any dinosaurs or flying saucers or flying dog bowls.

The Apollo 11 astronauts, like all astronauts, ate specially prepared space food. The food had to be lightweight and eaten out of tubes and packets.

Unless the food was packed tightly and securely, hotdogs might float around the capsule. In microgravity, any food floating around could have been dangerous.

Bread was banned in case crumbs floated about. Even drops of tomato juice could interfere with the workings of the spacecraft.

A lot of the food for space travel had to be preserved to stop it turning mouldy. This was done by freeze-drying which is a way to make sure it is still tasty. Before it was packed, the food was freeze-dried to make sure all the moisture was removed.

Some food could be eaten straight from the packages, such as brownie cubes. Other food needed to have hot or cold water added through a nozzle in the pack. Water guns were used for this.

After it was rehydrated with water, the astronauts could squeeze out the food straight into their mouths.

Best wishes,
Dr Isabella Starr
Rocket Scientist

PS It would be a bit splodgy
if tomato sauce floated around
the capsule and stuck to the
walls.

CHAPTER 3
Tomato Planets

Dr Isabella Starr
Rocket Scientist
Explore Space, UK

Dear Isabella,

That's really interesting about water guns.

Jasper now wants his food to be freeze-dried but I don't think he should be let loose with a water gun, especially not in Bogna Park.

It's also interesting what you say about splodgy tomato sauce. Jasper thinks that, if the rocket had got lost in space, and if aliens had found it, they might think we have tomato sauce wallpaper.

Jasper thinks the aliens might then try to grow tomatoes out there and that might cause problems.

Humans might wonder, when they look through their telescopes, why little red planets (which are really tomatoes) are suddenly floating about in space.

Jasper also thought that if they grew tomatoes they could grow wheat and make pizzas. Aliens could then deliver pizzas to anyone walking on the moon.

We have another question, well Jasper does. Jasper wants to know ...

did the astronauts see a man IN the moon?

If the astronauts did see a man **IN** the moon, did he go for a walk **ON** the moon, and did he have a dog?

If so, Jasper says, quite rightly, that Neil Armstrong would not have been the first man **ON** the moon.

The man **IN** the moon would have been the first **ON** the moon and our history books would be wrong. Well, Jasper doesn't have any history books but he borrows mine a lot.

Jasper is allowed in the library on 'Take Your Dog To Library Day' where he pretends to be interested. They let him walk about in there. He watches people working on the computer and acts as if he knows it all.

From Charlie Tanner, age 8
and a half, and Jasper, age
2 and a bit — well, actually,
he might be 3. We are not
sure and neither is he. Parrot
hasn't said anything at the
moment so we think he is
thinking about whether there is
a man in the moon. He keeps
looking up at it at night.

Dear Charlie Tanner,

We can assure you that the moonwalkers saw no evidence of a man living **IN** the moon. The Control Centre at Houston certainly never confirmed that.

On the 21st July 1969, Neil Armstrong was the first man to set foot **ON** the moon and said the famous words,

'That's one small step for a man, one giant leap for mankind.'

He said that because it was
the first time ever that a man
had stepped on the moon.

Buzz Aldrin was the second man on the moon. They landed in an area which they named 'Tranquility Base'. They travelled there in the lunar module which was called

'Eagle'.

Eagle had separated from the command module which was called 'Columbia' (the poetic name for America). When they landed the lunar module on the moon, Neil Armstrong said,

Houston, the Eagle has landed.

The third astronaut on that mission was Michael Collins but he stayed in the command module, Columbia, and continued to orbit the moon.

Best wishes,
Dr Isabella Starr
Rocket Scientist

PS If they had seen a man **IN** the moon I guess they would have rocketed away!

CHAPTER 4
Leaping Cows

Dr Isabella Starr
Rocket Scientist
Explore Space, UK

Dear Isabella,

Jasper has been thinking about Michael Collins flying around on his own and he would like to know ...

did Michael Collins see a cow?

Jasper's favourite song is the one about the cow that jumped over the moon.

If Michael Collins did see a cow, did it get in his way? It must be hard to dodge a cow in space.

Jasper has been thinking a lot about this. He says it would be really scary to be zooming around the moon in the dark and then suddenly see a leaping cow.

He thinks that if the cow pulled faces at the rocket window then Michael Collins might have flown the rocket away. Then the moonwalkers wouldn't have been able to get off the moon and might still be there! Well, that would be ok if there were 'pizza delivery aliens' but otherwise it might have been difficult to get them back to Earth.

We would also like to know why Michael Collins didn't walk on the moon as well? Were they cross with each other? That's what Jasper thinks. Jasper is always falling out with dogs over things such as bones and stuff.

At other times they just get along well and zoom about Bogna Park pretending to be dog rockets.

From Charlie Tanner, age 8
and a half, and Jasper, age
2 and a bit, maybe nearly 3,
but he acts as if he is 33
sometimes — well, he told me
to say that to you.

Dear Charlie Tanner,

Well, we can confirm that Apollo 11 did not crash into a cow in space!

Michael Collins flew on his own for almost 22 hours around the moon before reconnecting with the lunar module and the two moonwalkers.

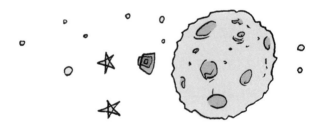

Michael Collins had to keep the command module going so they could all get back to Earth later.

There was no fall out as they were working together as a team. This plan was agreed before they left Earth.

Jasper might like to know that, on later space missions, astronauts were able to roam about the moon in a Lunar Roving Vehicle also known as a moon buggy.

Michael Collins was a superhero because he must have been a bit lonely being in a rocket on his own.

Best wishes,
Dr Isabella Starr
Rocket Scientist

CHAPTER 5
Chocolate-powered Rockets

Dr Isabella Starr
Rocket Scientist
Explore Space, UK

Dear Isabella,

Jasper thinks it's a shame there wasn't a rocket park on the moon for Michael Collins to park the rocket so he could have a walk too. He also thinks they should have been able to take it in turns to walk on the moon and they could have done this if there had been a rocket park there.

Jasper has found out that Buzz Aldrin was called Edwin when he was born. His sister couldn't say 'brother' and she called him 'Buzzer' and the name stuck!

Jasper likes this and he is wondering whether he should be called Jazzer or Jazz.

Jasper has worked out that Neil A, read backwards, spells Alien! He has also found out that Buzz Aldrin's mother's

surname before she was
married was 'Moon'.

Jasper is now thinking that
he might use the surname
'Everest' in case he has
puppies. Jasper Everest. Then
his puppies might feel they
want to climb Everest, the
highest mountain in the world.

Jasper has been reading about how great mountain climbers and walkers carry chocolate as 'emergency fuel' in case they run out of energy and he is wondering ...

could rockets be powered by chocolate?

I have to say, Isabella, that all this moon talk has gone to Jasper's head.

He now thinks he is a
rocket-scientist-in-the-making
and is strutting about the
room in his space boots acting
as if he has solved all the
world's problems.

I keep trying to get Jasper to play games and all he does is sit with a thoughtful face as if he's the brainiest dog in the world.

Parrot is silent at the moment. I think he is trying to work out how to say 'Jazz'.

From Charlie Tanner,
age 8 and a half, and Jasper,
who now wants to be called
Jazz the Space Dog.

Dear Charlie Tanner,

I read out your letter to the team here and we all found it very funny.

Then we thought about the idea and decided it might be a good plan to consider chocolate as a form of fuel for rockets.

If Jasper — or Jazzer — or Jazz – can come up with a design and details of how explosive chocolate might power a rocket, we would be delighted to consider it.

We could then include him as a key member of our team on our next mission.

Best wishes,
Dr Isabella Starr
Rocket Scientist

CHAPTER 6
One Small Step for a Dog

Dr Isabella Starr
Rocket Scientist
Explore Space, UK

Dear Isabella,

Jasper is considering his future. Parrot just sits and stares at him.

From Charlie Tanner, age 8 and a half, and Jasper, who is thinking about how old he ought to be.

Dr Isabella Starr
Rocket Scientist
Explore Space, UK

Dear Isabella,

After a lot of thought, Jazz
is unsure whether he just
wants to be a rocket scientist
dog. (I told you it has gone to
his head.) You see, Jazz is the
most ambitious dog I have ever
met. There are lots of things
that he would like to do,
such as climb to the top of
Everest and be the next Prime
Minister.

I just tell him, 'One thing at a time Jazz, one thing at a time.'

So now we know that:

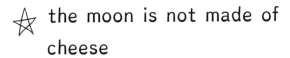 the moon is not made of cheese

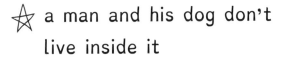 a man and his dog don't live inside it

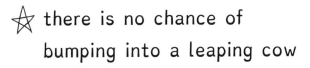 there is no chance of bumping into a leaping cow

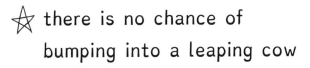 and Jazz can launch his rocket from Bogna Park in front of an audience of dogs.

He is wondering if you could help him make history? Do you think Jazz could become a superhero like Neil Armstrong by being the first dog to walk on the moon?

Do you think that he could take a buggy with him to zoom across the moon and look at all the planets as well?

He would like to name the buggy after Bogna Park – so it would be called ...

'The Bogna Buggy'

Jasper has been thinking about what he might call the command module. He thinks it should be called 'Britannia' (the poetic name for Great Britain). He also wants to call his lunar module 'Parrot'. Parrot seems to like this idea.

Jasper has been practising the words,

> **That's one small step for a dog, one giant leap for dogkind.**

and he keeps saying,

> **Bogna, the Parrot has landed!**

If you think it is possible
for a dog to make history,
please could you, in all future
letters, address him as

**Jazz, Space Dog
on a Mission.**

From Charlie Tanner, age 8
and a half, and Jazz, Space
Dog on a Mission.

CHAPTER 7
Mission Accomplished

Dear Jazz,

Space Dog
on a Mission

The team here at Explore Space would like to offer you a job as part of our team.

Best wishes,
Dr Isabella Starr
Rocket Scientist
(age 36 and a half)

JAZZ!

Space Dog on a Mission

Bogna Superhero!

CHAPTER 8

Mission Facts with Jasper

Jasper has found out all kinds of exciting facts about the Apollo 11 space mission. Here are a few of his favourites:

☆ At first, the Apollo 11 scientists wanted to call their spacecraft Snowcone and Haystack instead of Columbia and Eagle! Jasper thinks it would have been funny if Neil Armstrong had said, 'Houston the Haystack has landed!'

☆ The Apollo 11 crew couldn't
afford life insurance so Neil,
Buzz and Michael signed
hundreds of autographs
and sent them to a friend.
The plan was to sell the
autographs if they didn't make
it home so that there would
be enough money to look after
their families. Jasper says
he is always being asked for
signed photos from dogs in
Bogna Park.

☆ It took four days to reach
the moon. Apollo 11 was
launched on the 16th July 1969

and the first ever moonwalk took place on 21st July. They splashed down in Hawaii on the 24th July.

☆ Eagle was due to land on a flat patch on the moon called 'Tranquility Base' but instead it headed towards a crater that was the size of a football pitch! It was full of rocks and boulders. It would have been dangerous to land there so Neil Armstrong kept calm and took over the controls to park Eagle manually. It was a scary moment!

Jasper would like to play football on the moon but not in a crater in case he can't get out. Golf was once played on the moon by astronauts involved in a later mission.

☆ At the point where Eagle eventually touched down on Tranquility Base there was only 25 seconds of fuel left! Jasper shakes every time he thinks of this.

☆ Buzz and Neil were meant to take a nap once they landed on the moon, but they were so keen to explore that the controllers gave them permission to skip it. Jasper is getting a sleeping spacebag made to camp out on the moon!

☆ Moon dust got trapped in the creases of the astronauts' spacesuits. When they were back in the rocket there was a strange smell. They realised it came from the moon dust mixing with oxygen in the rocket. The astronauts thought it smelled like gunpowder.

☆ After gathering their rock samples, Buzz and Neil realised that an important circuit switch had broken in their capsule. This meant they couldn't get off the moon! They were supposed to sleep while the controllers worked out what to do. While they were waiting, Buzz jammed his pen into the mechanism to fix it and it worked! They were able to rocket off the moon and join up again with Michael Collins in Columbia. Jasper is taking Charlie's pens with him, just in case.

☆ President Nixon knew there was a chance that the astronauts might not come back from the moon if something went wrong. It was a worrying time for their families, for everyone involved and for the watching world. The President had written a speech which read, 'Fate has ordained that the men who went to the moon to explore in peace still stay on the moon to rest in peace.' He also had another speech ready to read and, as we now know, that was all that was needed! Charlie Tanner has written a speech to celebrate Jasper's achievement should he be the first dog to walk on the moon.

⭐ Despite being mega famous, the astronauts, like all tourists, still had to fill out a customs form when they entered Hawaiian territory! In the part that asks where people have travelled from, they wrote, 'The Moon'.

⭐ When the astronauts were back on Earth, they were kept apart from other people. This meant that they couldn't be in contact with anyone for 21 days in case of any moon diseases! In later years it was found there were no diseases that could be caught from the moon. Parrot keeps saying, 'Moonbug, moonbug, who's caught a moonbug!'

☆ Much of the success of several Apollo missions was due to the work of many experts, including Katherine Johnson who was described as a 'human calculator'. Jasper would like Parrot to learn maths. Parrot just says, 'Silly boy, silly boy'.

CHAPTER 9
Space Facts with Jasper

Jasper has been finding out how years of development in space technology has changed life on Earth today. Here are a few of his favourite space facts.

☆ Charlie Tanner and Jasper are always taking selfies thanks to camera phones which were originally developed to fit comfortably inside astronauts' space suits. Parrot likes to photobomb their selfies.

☆ To prevent rocks, dirt and
   small particles scratching the
   visors on astronauts' helmets,
   scientists found a way to
   create 'scratch resistant
   lenses'. This technology led
   to improvements in today's
   eyewear. Jasper reminds
   Charlie Tanner of this every
   time he puts on his sunglasses.

☆ Jasper likes to run around
   Bogna Park in his space
   boots and now we know why!
   Astronauts really did have a
   spring in their step and that

wasn't just because they were excited to be jumping around on the moon. The boots they wore were specially designed to protect their feet from extreme weather conditions and sharp rocks. That technology led to improvements in sports shoes and Jasper now plans to run a marathon. 🐾 🐾 🐾 🐾

⭐ Charlie Tanner needed to wear braces and his dentist told him that if it wasn't for space exploration we might not have the material that is

now used for invisible braces.
Jasper would like to wear
a brace but Charlie says he
doesn't need one. Parrot keeps
saying, 'Space brace'.

☆ There's no electricity on the
moon (yet) so drilling for rocks
would be difficult without
battery-charged cordless
tools, which were developed
by scientists to help the
astronauts. Jasper is thinking
of all the things we use
electricity for, like a hairdryer,
and would like to invent one
to take to the moon.

Charlie has told him that he would look ridiculous drying his fur in space.

☆ Satellites have helped us to predict the weather, communicate over the internet, make long distance phone calls, watch television and show us how to get from place to place without paper maps. Jasper wonders if a rocket satnav might help him find his way to other planets and travel where 'no dog has gone before'!

☆ Meanwhile, footprints left by Neil Armstrong and Buzz Aldrin still, today, remain at Tranquility Base.

Jasper is hoping to leave a pawprint there too.

JASPER – Viking Dog!

The next book in the series of
the Misadventures of Jasper.

Jasper believes he may descend from a long line of Viking dogs and is keen to help out at the local Viking museum.

The second book in the Misadventures of Jasper series, sees Jasper, Charlie Tanner and Astrid the Curator, explore interesting and hilarious ways in which Jasper might help to attract visitors.

The picture (opposite) is the official photograph of the Apollo 11 Prime Crew.

From left to right:

Neil Armstrong (Commander)

Michael Collins (Command Module Pilot)

Edwin (Buzz) Aldrin (Lunar Module Pilot)

The third man to walk on the moon, Pete Conrad (Apollo 12) overcame the challenges posed by dyslexia to become one of NASA's most travelled astronauts.

Photograph: BC03M3 Apollo 11 Astronauts

Contributor: The Print Collector/Alamy
Stock Photo

STRAUSS HOUSE
PRODUCTIONS

www.strausshouseproductions.com